CANTI
cath

CW00922872

A Paines Plough and **Canterbury Festival**
production of

Dallas Sweetman

by Sebastian Barry

A Commission by Canterbury Cathedral
and Canterbury Festival
with Paines Plough

The first performance of *Dallas Sweetman* took place
on 24 September 2008 in Canterbury Cathedral

Supported by

D'Oyly Carte Charitable Trust, The Ernest Cook Trust,
Canterbury Christ Church University, University of Kent,
The King's School, The Tory Foundation

Patron
The Most Rev'd & Rt Hon Rowan Williams, Archbishop of Canterbury

A Message from the Commissioners

I was chatting to the Archdeacon one day after matins, in the Dark Entry, as we often do. The conversation led on to the forthcoming Festival, and we reflected that the original link between the Cathedral, faith and drama had died away.

At first we talked of an open competition for scripts, but fortunately we were then joined by the professionalism of Rosie Turner and the Canterbury Festival Office who advised commissioning. The Festival in turn brought Paines Plough on board. Four years later we are all here, delighted that Sebastian Barry's *Dallas Sweetman* is to be performed.

Whilst the plan for the play's production developed, the original concept remained. We were seeking a play which explored faith rather than one which was didactic. We wanted a play which asked questions as much as it provided answers. The first Canterbury Plays were about the history of events related to the Cathedral: they were about Becket's life and martyrdom, Cranmer or the Peasants' Revolt. We wanted to move away from this. *Dallas Sweetman's* treatment of the Becket story is very different from those earlier treatments. A small but important point was that we also looked for a play which had significant roles for women.

Dallas Sweetman explores significant themes in Christian tradition and experience: human and divine judgement, and the possibility of redemption and forgiveness; as well as the nature of truth and memory.

Canon Edward Condry
Canterbury Cathedral, 2008

The Friends of Canterbury Cathedral was founded in 1927 by the distinguished scholar and poet Dean George Allen Kennedy Bell who later became Bishop of Chichester. In 1928 Miss Margaret Babington joined Dean Bell as Steward of The Friends. A redoubtable woman of enormous energy and tremendous vision, she made a huge contribution to the success of the charity. She enticed famous people to write plays for the early Friends' Festivals of Music and Drama – writers such as John Masefield, Dorothy L. Sayers and T. S. Eliot, who wrote the most celebrated of the plays *Murder in the Cathedral*.

The Friends today are the Cathedral's fan club. Our members are admirers of the building, its history and its life. They are an integral part of the Cathedral and its community and work with the Dean & Chapter to help preserve it for ever. Over the years The Friends have contributed millions of pounds to help support the buildings, ornaments, furnishings and the life of the Cathedral.

We are very pleased to help revive the illustrious tradition of commissioning cathedral plays established in the early years of the charity with our sponsorship of this new cathedral play *Dallas Sweetman* by Sebastian Barry.

Pam Doyle
Executive Secretary, 20 August 2008

Canterbury Festival

Kent's International Arts Festival
11–25 October 2008

*Bringing the best of the world to Canterbury
and showing the best of Canterbury to the rest of the world*

The Canterbury Festival takes place each October staging two hundred events in two weeks in venues throughout the historic city. Famous for its Cathedral concerts and international music programme, recent Festivals have seen an increase in theatre production, especially of new work of specific relevance to East Kent.

Promised Land – an opera about the decline of the Kent coalfields – was commissioned and produced in 2006 and involved over 150 members of the community in rehearsals for over a year.

Dallas Sweetman reinvigorates the tradition of new Cathedral Plays from which the Festival originated in the late 1920s and heralds the way for the 75th anniversary revival of T S Eliot's *Murder in the Cathedral* in 2010.

The Canterbury Festival is supported by the Arts Council, Kent County Council and Canterbury City Council. Its Principal Sponsor is Canterbury Christ Church University and its Media Partners are Classic FM and the Kentish Gazette.

The Canterbury Festival is also indebted to its corporate sponsors, individual patrons and one thousand Friends whose energy and loyalty allow the Festival to flourish and serve a wider and more diverse community each year.

For further information about the Festival,
to join the Friends or the free mailing list visit
www.canterburyfestival.co.uk

Festival Director	Rosie Turner
Marketing Manager	Megan Williams
Development Manager	Amanda McKean
Festival Administrator	Sylviane Martell
Finance Manager	John Biffin
Programme Assistant	John Prebble

Special thanks to Louise Griffiths and David Everett

Executive Producers for the Cathedral Plays Series
Rosie Turner, Canterbury Festival
Canon Edward Condry, Canterbury Cathedral

Paines Plough is an award-winning, nationally and internationally renowned theatre company, specialising exclusively in commissioning and producing new plays.

> *'The ever-inventive Paines Plough.'*
> (The Independent)

Inspired by the creativity of our writers we've embraced the challenge of seeking the most exciting spaces in which to produce our work. Our international footprint is far-reaching: our productions have recently been seen late at night in the depths of London's West End; over lunch on the South Bank; in St. Petersburg and Bradford, New York and Plymouth; in railway vaults and disused coal houses, on the Globe Stage, at the Edinburgh Festival and in a cupboard in Brighton.

> *'Paines Plough's nomadic theatre company*
> *has racked up so many stars that browsing its press release*
> *is a bit like looking into deep space.'* (Metro)

Alongside our creation of some of the UK's most thrilling productions, we work to develop and encourage the very best of the new generation of writers. Activities include our flagship scheme for emerging writers, Future Perfect, and our late night salon Later.

> *'Some of the most exciting theatre in the UK.'* (The Guardian)

We continue to seek out partners with whom we can collaborate in a bold, responsive spirit to generate new plays that engage with the contemporary world. Paines Plough is thrilled to be working with Canterbury Festival and Canterbury Cathedral to bring this exciting new commission into production.

Paines Plough are:

Artistic Director	Roxana Silbert
General Manager	Anneliese Davidsen
Literary Director	Tessa Walker
Administrative Assistant	Livvy Morris
Book-Keeper	Wojtek Trzcinski
Pearson Playwright	Duncan Macmillan

Board of Directors: Ola Animashawun, Tamara Cizeika, Giles Croft, David Edwards, Chris Elwell, Fraser Grant, Marilyn Imrie, Clare O'Brien, Jenny Sealey

To find out more or to join our mailing list visit www.painesplough.com

Paines Plough is supported by the Arts Council England

Paines Plough has the support of the Pearson Playwrights' scheme sponsored by Pearson plc and of Channel 4 for our Future Perfect programme.

A Paines Plough and
Canterbury Festival Production

Dallas Sweetman

by Sebastian Barry

Dallas Sweetman	**Conleth Hill**
Mrs Reddan	**Bríd Brennan**
Lucinda	**Lisa Hogg**
Lucius	**David Sibley**
Sister, Elizabeth I, Princess of Brazil, and Ensemble	**Jillian Bradbury**
Director	**Roxana Silbert**
Designer	**Robert Innes Hopkins**
Lighting Designer	**Chahine Yavroyan**
Composer	**Mark Dougherty**
Sound Designer	**George Glossop**
Assistant Director	**Luke Kernaghan**
Casting Advisor	**Amy Ball**
Producer	**Emma Dunton**
Press	**Sharon Kean** for Kean | Lanyon
Production Manager	**Simon Byford**
Stage Manager	**Christabel Anderson**
Stage Manager	**Eavan Murphy**
Wardrobe Supervisor	**Sian Harris**
ASM Intern	**Naomi Young**

Musicians

Guitars: **Johnny Scott**
Pipes, Whistles, Bodhran & Bones: **Brendan Monaghan**
Organ: **John Robinson**
The Choristers of Canterbury Cathedral, directed by **David Flood**

Technical Crew

Chief Electrician	**Ian Brown**
Electricians	**Rachel Shipp, Ed Trotter**
Sound Engineers	**Fergus Mount, Charlie Dorman**
Stage Carpenter	**Peter Walleitner**
Assistant to Simon Byford	**Philippa Smith**
Set built by	**Simon York** at Miraculous Engineering
Set painted by	**Kerry Jarrett**
Lighting supplied by	**PRG Europe Ltd**
Sound supplied by	**Dimension**, a part of Creative Technology Ltd

With special thanks to the Dean and Chapter of Canterbury and staff;
Matthew Cole at Glyndebourne Opera; Jon Cadbury at PRG;
Ushi Bagga, Pippa Ellis, Cathy King

Cast

Jillian Bradbury | Lucius's Sister/Elizabeth I/Princess of Brazil/
Ensemble

Jillian graduated from RADA in July 2008.

Film includes: *Winter's End* – independent feature film in association with The
Irish Film Board, directed by Patrick Kenny.

Jillian won the Gate Theatre Award in 2001 and was nominated for Best
Actress at the Irish Film and Television Awards 2005.

Bríd Brennan | Mrs Reddan

Theatre includes: *Doubt* (Abbey Theatre, Dublin), *Dancing at Lughnasa* (Tony
Award winner, Abbey Theatre Dublin/National Theatre & Phoenix Theatre
London/Plymouth Theatre/Broadway), *Silver Birch House* (Arcola Theatre), *The
Cosmonaut's Last Message to the Woman he Once Loved in the Former Soviet
Union, The Dark, The Little Foxes* (Olivier Award Nomination) (Donmar
Warehouse), *A Kind of Alaska* (Donmar Warehouse/Lincoln Centre NYC),
Playboy of the Western World (Druid Theatre Co.,Galway/Irish Tour/Donmar
Warehouse), *Smelling a Rat* (Hampstead Theatre), *Intemperance* (Liverpool
Everyman), *Edward II* (Manchester Royal Exchange), *Pillars of the Community,
Rutherford & Son* (Olivier Award Nomination) (National Theatre), *Brendan at
The Chelsea* (Riverside Studios), *Bailegangaire, Bliss, Bone, Woman and
Scarecrow* (Royal Court Theatre), *La Lupa, Macbeth* (RSC), *Holy Days* (Time
Out Award, Soho Poly), *Ten Rounds* (Tricycle), *Absolutely, Perhaps, By The Bog
of Cats* (Wyndhams).

Television includes: *Any Time Now, Ballroom of Romance, The Billy Trilogy,
Cracker III, The Daily Woman, Four Days in July, The Hidden City, Lorna,
Sunday, Tell Tale Hearts, Trial & Retribution.*

Film includes: *Anne Devlin, Dancing At Lughnasa* (IFTA Best Actress 1999),
Felicia's Journey, Guinevere, Maeve Trojan Eddie, Ursula and Glenys.

Radio includes: *84 Charing Cross Road, The Subtle Knife* and *The Amber Spyglass.*

Conleth Hill | Dallas Sweetman

Theatre includes: *Philistines* (Olivier Award Nominee), *The Producers* (Olivier
Award Winner), *The Seafarer* (Drama Desk Award, Tony Nominee), *Democracy,
Shoot the Crow, Stones in his Pockets* (Olivier Award, Drama Desk Award
& Tony Nominee), *Conversations on a Homecoming, Waiting for Godot,
Whistle in the Dark, Little Shop of Horrors, The Iceman Cometh, Importance
of Being Earnest, Playboy of the Western World, Midsummer Night's Dream*
(Lyric Belfast), *Northern Star* (Tinderbox), *A Christmas Carol, The Suicide*
(Communicado), *Picture of Dorian Gray, School for Wives* (Ulster Theatre),
After Darwin, Endgame (Primecut).

Television includes: *Blue Heaven, Goodbye Mr Chips, The Life and Times of
Vivienne Vyle,* Peter Kay's Pop Factor, *Meaningful Sex.*

Film includes: Woody Allen's *Whatever Works, Intermission, Cycle of Violence,
Man You Don't Meet Every Day, Out of the Deep Pan, Trust Me.*

Lisa Hogg | Lucinda

Theatre includes: *Many Loves* (Lilian Baylis), *The Fisherking*, *War of Words* (Lyric Theatre, Belfast), *Pete and Me* (New End), *Begin Again* (Old Vic, 24 Hour Plays), *Loyal Women* (Royal Court), *War Crimes Tribunal* (Soho), *Tarmacking the Belt/Waxing and Waning* (Soho Theatre/Theatre Works), *Much Ado About Nothing* (Stafford Shakespeare Festival), *In the Jungle of the City* (Windsor Arts Centre / Drill Hall).

Television includes: *The Bill, Casualty, Commander, Fallen, The Royal, Trial & Retribution, Wire in the Blood*.

Film includes: Julie Taymor's *Across the Universe*, Yousaf Ali Khan's *Almost Adult*.

Radio includes: *Loyal Women* (BBC World Service).

David Sibley | Lucius

Theatre includes: *King Lear* (Almeida), *Naked* (Almeida & West End), *Project E – An Explosion* (BAC), *The Last Elephant, Turning Over* (Bush), *Beckett's Words and Music* (Birmingham Contemporary Music Group), *A Midsummer Night's Dream* (Bristol Old Vic), *Belonging* (Cheltenham Festival), *Ripped* (Cockpit), *Dirty Wonderland, Rabbit* (Frantic Assembly), *The Great Highway* (Gate), *Lion in the Streets* (Hampstead), *Absolute Beginners* (Lyric Theatre), *The Marriage of Mr Mississippi* (New End), *Some Explicit Polaroids* (Out of Joint & West End), *Positive Hour* (Out of Joint & Hampstead), *Space Race* (RSC in Davidson, North Carolina), *Hamlet* (Royal Court), Edward Bond's *Lear* (Sheffield Crucible), *Playing God, Moby Dick* (Stephen Joseph Theatre, Scarborough), *Cocks and Hens* (Soho Poly), *Cruel and Tender* (Young Vic and European Tour), and repertory in Chester, Exeter and Leeds.

Television includes: *A&E, An Inspector Calls, Attachments, The Big One, Care, Casualty, The Commander II, Doctors, Drovers Gold, Emmerdale, The Fatal Spring, Frontiers, Fun at the Funeral Parlour, Holby City, Judge John Deed, The Kitchen, Love Again, Middlemarch, Newborn, The Nightmare Years, Redemption, Stars of the Roller State Disco, Traitors, Trial and Retribution, Voyage of the Beagle, Wilderness Road, The Year That London Blew Up, Young Indy*.

Film includes: *Dangerous Parking, Ghandi, Guest House Paradiso, Heartless, Hinterland, Incognito, Princess Cariboo, Willow, Yanks*.

Radio includes: *Feed Me, The Front Page, Naked, Text Message, The True Memoirs of Harriet Wilson*.

Company

Christabel Anderson | Stage Manager

Christabel trained at The University of Edinburgh and LAMDA.

Previous work for Paines Plough: *After The End* (National and International Tour), *Strawberries In January* (Traverse Theatre), and *Wild Lunch* (Young Vic Theatre).

Other credits include: two seasons as Resident Stage Manager at the Bush Theatre and plays for the West Yorkshire Playhouse, Hampstead Theatre, Nabokov and Out of Joint. She has also worked on pantomimes at the Cambridge Arts and Richmond Theatres and on opera festivals at Wexford, Garsington, Grange Park and Longborough. Her next project is a double bill of new plays for the Traverse Theatre and the National Theatre of Scotland.

Christabel was nominated for the SMA award in 2007.

Sebastian Barry | Writer

Sebastian Barry was born in Dublin in 1955 and educated at Trinity College Dublin. He was Writer Fellow there in 1996. He was also Writer in Association at the Abbey Theatre in 1990, and recently held the Heimbold Visiting Chair in Irish Studies at Villanova University in the USA. His plays include *Boss Grady's Boys* (Abbey 1988), *The Steward of Christendom* (1995, which played London and New York and toured internationally with Out-of-Joint theatre company), and *Our Lady of Sligo* (1998, London, Dublin and New York, Out-of-Joint).

His theatre awards include the BBC/Stewart Parker Award (1989), the Christopher Ewart-Biggs Memorial Prize, the Ireland/America Literary Prize, the Critics' Circle Award for Best New Play, the Writers' Guild Award, the Lloyds Private Banking Playwright of the Year Award and the Peggy Ramsay Play Award (jointly), as well as a nomination for the Olivier Award.

Sebastian has also published several works of poetry and fiction, including the novels *The Whereabouts of Eneas McNulty* (Picador 1998), *Annie Dunne* (Faber and Faber 2002) and *A Long Long Way* (Faber and Faber 2005) which was short-listed for the Booker Prize 2005 and the International Dublin Impac Prize, and won the Kerry Group Irish Fiction Award. His new novel *The Secret Scripture* (Faber and Faber, 2008) is long-listed for the Booker Prize 2008.

Sebastian Barry's most recent play *The Pride of Parnell Street* was nominated for an *Irish Times* Irish Theatre Award for Best Play. It opened in London in 2007, and played the Dublin Theatre Festival; and toured to France, Germany, and the US this year.

Simon Byford | Production Manager

Simon has been working in the performing arts industry for 30 years. He has collaborated with many different producers, working predominantly as a Production Manager.

Previous work with: Dance Umbrella, Adam Cooper, Adventures in Motion Pictures and New Adventures, Rosie Lee, Merce Cunningham, Mark Morris in the Dance world, Opera Factory, Raymond Gubbay, Royal College of Music, London Sinfonietta, Philharmonia Orchestra, London Philharmonic Orchestra, Pimlico Opera and Garsington Opera in the opera world, Islington International Festival, Brighton Festival, Artsfest Birmingham, Japan Festival 2001 in Hyde Park, Larmer Tree Festival, Big Chill and many other festivals around the UK.

Simon has worked in theatre with The Royal Court, ICA, Kathy Burke, Francis Mathews, Joint Stock and several West End producers.

Site-specific shows and non theatre venues are very much Simon's speciality.

Emma Dunton | Producer

Emma has recently become a freelance theatre producer following seven years as Executive Director of ATC. Recent credits include: *The Brothers Size* by Tarell Alvin McCraney (Young Vic/Olivier nomination), *Bad Jazz* by Bob Farquhar (Theatre Royal Plymouth/tour), *Gizmo Love* by John Kolvenbach (Assembly Rooms/tour), *A Brief History of Helen of Troy* by Mark Schultz (Soho Theatre/tour), *Country Music* and *One Minute* by Simon Stephens (Royal Court /Bush Theatre). Previously Emma has worked for Volcano theatre company, the British Council and on feature films in Los Angeles.

Mark Dougherty | Composer

Mark has been composing music for theatre, radio and television for twenty-five years. His most notable scores include *Kentish Tales* (2007) and *Promised Land* (2006) – for Canterbury Festival, *The Belfast Carmen* (2003) and *With One Voice* (2000) – for The Ulster Orchestra, *Probable Cause* (2002) – for Channel Five TV, *Connections* (2001) – for Belfast Festival, *Traditional Sounds* (1998) – for BBC2, and *Murder in the Cathedral* (1996) – for Ulster Theatre Company.

He has written six musicals all of which have been staged, and has just presented the first half of his seventh – *The Chosen Room* – co written with Marie Jones (*Stones in His Pockets*, *Women on the Verge of HRT*), as a work in progress.

As a musical director and musician Mark has worked with Van Morrison, Suzi Quatro, Shane MacGowan, Johnny Mathis, as a studio musician for Don Williams in Nashville, and has directed the music for most of the well known musicals including *West Side Story* and *Oklahoma* UK tours. He was musical director for *Riverdance* from 2000 – 2004, and October this year sees him touring a new show – *Celtic Thunder* (currently the no. 2 best-selling DVD) - in America. He has produced nine albums for various artists.

George Glossop | Sound Designer

George is a freelance audio designer and engineer and co-founder and director of Hardware House (Sound) Ltd.

His previous experience includes work with Crucible Theatre, Sheffield; Arts Theatre, Ipswich; Shaw Theatre, London and Royal Exchange, Manchester. He has also been a course tutor at Aberystwyth University Theatre and was senior engineer and system designer at Dimension Audio Ltd.

Sian Harris | Wardrobe Supervisor

Sian trained at the London College of Fashion, and has worked in the theatre for over 20 years.

She has been a costume maker as well as a wardrobe mistress for many West End shows. As a costume supervisor she has worked on projects for theatre, opera, dance, circus and corporate clients and has two long-standing engagements with the National Opera Studio and the Lord Mayor's Show. She has also been head of costume for the National Youth Theatre for three years. Other recent work includes the *Magic Flute, A Night at the Chinese Opera* and *The Marriage of Figaro* (Royal Academy of Music), *White Boy* (Soho Theatre) *and I Saw Myself* (Wrestling School).

Robert Innes Hopkins | Designer

Recent theatre includes: *Twelfth Night, Romeo and Juliet* (Open Air Theatre, Regent's Park), *The Member of the Wedding* (The Young Vic), *The Pain and the Itch* (Royal Court), *Our Country's Good* (Liverpool Playhouse), *Pinocchio* (Royal Lyceum Theatre Edinburgh), *Carousel* (Chichester), *Promises Promises* (TMA Best Design Award Winner, Crucible Theatre, Sheffield), *Julius Caesar* (Royal Lyceum Theatre Edinburgh), *The Resistible Rise of Arturo Ui (starring Al Pacino,* National Actors Theatre New York,) *The Malcontent* (RSC & West End), *Redundant* (Royal Court).

Other Work Includes: *The Servant of Two Masters, Comedy of Errors* (RSC), *Romeo and Juliet, The Villain's Opera* (National Theatre).

Most recent opera productions include: *Billy Budd* (Santa Fe Opera), *Lohengrin* (Geneva Opera), *Carmen* (The Bolshoi Opera), *Die Soldaten* (Ruhr Triennale & Lincoln Centre Festival), *Betrothal In A Monastery* (Glyndebourne & Valencia), *Cavalleria Rusticana, Pagliacci* (Deutsche Oper Berlin), *The Flying Dutchman* (Opernhaus Zurich and Welsh National Opera), *The Cunning Little Vixen* (The Bregenz Festival, San Francisco & Geneva), *Rigoletto* (The Welsh National Opera), *The Elixir Of Love* (Opera North & Welsh National Opera), *Peter Grimes, Italiana in Algeri*, Wozzeck (Santa Fe Opera), *Paradise Moscow* (Opera North).

Luke Kernaghan | Assistant Director

A graduate of Oxford University and the Ecole Internationale de Théâtre Jacques Lecoq in Paris, Luke gained an MA in directing from Central School of Speech and Drama and trained at the National Theatre Studio.

Directing includes: *Huis Clos Tango (From Here to Malaysia: Live Shorts)* (Soho Theatre), *The B File* (Etcetera), *The Rover* (Etcetera).

As Movement Director: *Certified Male (U.K. premiere,* Edinburgh).

Assistant Director: David Glass Ensemble's *Gormenghast* (BAC and national tour), *The Kaos Dream* (national tour).

Luke is also the co-translator of Lecoq's *Theatre of Movement and Gesture* and David Bradby's *History of French Theatre,* as well as a visiting lecturer at various institutes including Central School of Speech of Drama.

Luke is Associate Director of the David Glass ensemble and was a finalist for the 2008 JMK Young Director's Award.

Eavan Murphy | Stage Manager

After completing a course in Art and Design, Eavan studied Theatre Production at Colaiste Stiofan Naofa in Cork. She has recently returned from the international tour of Sebastian Barry's *The Pride of Parnell Street*.

Other credits include: *La Traviata* (Opera Ireland), *Improbable Frequency* (including Edinburgh Festival and Kontakt Festival in Poland),*The Bonefire* (Rough Magic Theatre Company), *The Barber of Seville* (Opera Theatre Company), three Irish tours of *I Keano* (Lane Productions), *Madame T* (Meridian Theatre Company), The Train Show (Cork Midsummer Festival), *The Little Mermaid* (Big Telly Productions), *The Nutcracker* (The Point Theatre Company), and *The Podge and Rodge Show* (Double Z Productions).

Roxana Silbert | Director

Roxana has been Artistic Director of Paines Plough Theatre Company since April 2005, and became an Associate Director at the RSC in 2008. She was Literary Director at the Traverse Theatre (2001-2004) and Associate Director, Royal Court (1998-2000). In 1997, Roxana was Associate Director of West Yorkshire Playhouse where she directed *Precious* by Anna Reynolds.

Theatre includes: *Shoot/Get Treasure/Repeat* (Paines Plough), *Strawberries in January* (Paines Plough /Traverse Theatre), *Long Time Dead* (Paines Plough/ Plymouth Theatre Royal), *Under The Black Flag* (Globe), *After The End* (Paines Plough/Bush UK and international tour), *Whistle in the Dark* (Citizens Theatre, Glasgow), *Blond Bombshells* (West Yorkshire Playhouse), *Property* (RNT Studio), *Damages* (Bush Theatre), *The Slab Boys, Still Life from The Slab Boys Trilogy* (Traverse Theatre/national tour),*The People Next Door* (Traverse Theatre/Theatre Royal, Stratford East); *Iron* (Traverse Theatre/Royal Court), *Brixton Stories* (RSC), *The Price* (Octagon Theatre, Bolton) *Top Girls, Translations* (New Vic Theatre, Stoke), *Cadillac Ranch* (Soho Theatre), *At the Table, Still Nothing, I Was So Lucky, Been So Long, Fairgame, Bazaar, Sweetheart* (Royal Court), *Mules* (Royal Court/Clean Break Theatre Company national tour), *Splash Hatch on the E* (Donmar Warehouse), *Write Away, Ice Station H.I.P.P.O* (Channel 4 Sitcom Festival at Riverside Studios), *Fast Show Live* (Hammersmith Apollo/tour), *The Treatment* (Intercity Theatre, Festival, Florence).

Radio includes: *Billiards* by Heinrich Böll adapted by Claire Luckham, *Japanese Gothic Tales* by Georgia Pritchard, *The Tall One* by Claire Luckham, *The Tape Recorded Highlights of a Humble Bee* by Brendan O'Casey, *The Good Father* by Christian O'Reilly (all for BBC Radio 4), *Brace Position* by Rona Munro for BBC Radio Scotland.

Chahine Yavroyan | Lighting Designer

Previous work with Paines Plough - *House of Agnes, Long Time Dead, After the End.*

Recent theatre work includes: *Three Sisters* (Manchester Royal Exchange) *Relocated* (Royal Court Upstairs), *Ghost Sonata* (The People Show), *Strawberries in January, Damascus* and *When the Bulbul Stopped Singing* (Traverse), *The Wonderful World of Dissocia, Realism, Elizabeth Gordon Quinn* and *San Diego* (National Theatre of Scotland), *Mahabharata* (Sadler's Wells),

God in Ruins (RSC at Soho), *Il Tempo del Postino* (Manchester International Festival), *There's Only One Waine Matthews* (Polka Theatre), *Ornamental Happiness* (Unity Theatre), *How to Live* (Barbican Theatre) and *Othello* (Nottingham Playhouse).

Recent dance work with: Jasmin Vardimon, Candoco, Frauke Requardt Dance, Bock & Vincenzi, Ricochet, Arthur Pita's Open Heart, Hofesh Schechter.

Site-specific work includes: *Enchanted Parks, Dreams of a Winter Night, Deep End* and *Spa* for Geraldine Pilgrim and *Light Touch* (Scarabeus).

Music work includes: *Dalston Songs* (ROH2), *Plague Songs* (Barbican Hall), *The Death of Klinghoffer* (EIF) and The Jocelyn Pook Ensemble (Thames Festival).

Naomi Young | Assistant Stage Manager

Naomi has just graduated from the Central School of Speech and Drama studying Stage Management.

Her recent freelance work includes Stage Manager for *The Stone Garden* (Swiss Cottage Fountain), Company Stage Manager for *Slippery Mountain* (New World Restaurant Soho London), Production Manager for *Sarajevo Story* (Lyric Studio Hammersmith), Props Buyer for *The Juniper Tree* (South of England Tour), Stage Manager for outdoor performances in Liverpool European City of Culture, Assistant Stage Manager for *The Tinderbox* (Albany Theatre) and *Sweeney Todd* (Shawford Mill) Props Buyer for *Take Flight* (Menier Chocolate Factory), Stage Manager for *Back At You* (BAC), *The Near Distance* (Lyric Studio Hammersmith), *The Arden of Faversham* (The White Bear Theatre) and *My Life* (Croydon Warehouse).

Sebastian Barry
Dallas Sweetman

ff

faber and faber

First published in 2008
by Faber and Faber Limited
3 Queen Square, London WC1N 3AU

Typeset by Country Setting, Kingsdown, Kent CT14 8ES
Printed in England by CPI Bookmarque, Croydon, Surrey

A CIP record for this book
is available from the British Library

978-0-571-24470-6

2 4 6 8 10 9 7 5 3 1

For Jean Kennedy Smith,
with friendship and love

Characters

Dallas Sweetman

Mrs Reddan

Lucinda

Lucius

Sister

Belinda

Servant

Elizabeth I

Princess of Brazil

Mountifort Longfield

This volume went to press before the end of rehearsals
so the text may differ slightly from the play as performed

DALLAS SWEETMAN

Act One

We hear the name 'Dallas Sweetman, Dallas Sweetman' called.

A man enters as if throwing off sleep.

He brings certain shadows with him unbeknownst, the shape of Mrs Reddan. The other characters of the play stir behind him, as if, when he moves, he pulls on a common web.

He is elderly enough, but spry, a servant of some standing in an Irish family, dressed in the grave-marked clothes of the 1600s.

Dallas Who calls me? I am that man, Dallas Sweetman.

No one, nothing, nil, forgotten.

He seems fearful, unsure.

I have lain three hundred years and more in that broken precinct of the yard, where no one goes. I am a little dusty from my grave. Forgive me. I would not choose to appear before you so. I have no brush to brush my jacket, no stone to rub my trews.

He looks out at the audience.

Was it ye called me? For what purpose? My name came floating on the air. As when in vanished years my father called me, and in I hurried from the stubbled fields, or my master, in those lost, loved days that indifferent time removed.

I greet you.

An Irish person of no account. Mere servant.

I do remember this particular, special place. I stood here with my good master, Lucius Lysaght, years beyond counting, on pilgrimage from Ireland. And when I was an old, old man, I came back here again, when all I knew were dead, hardly knowing why, to shrive myself and make my peace with God, and died impromptu on these stones, and was indifferently buried by the priests. Like a stain or morsel tidied away. No stone or marker given, only a dusty hole, and I was placed therein, and covered over.

And lay there like a story interrupted. Lacking a resolution and an ending.

Which is a type of sorrow to a soul.

Why have you called me now? Is there some rumour still of me, and of my life? I must doubt that. Is it God calls me, in God's great house?

Many sins lie on me, I know. Are they to devour me now, so late?

This is a place for soul trials, certainly.

The silence narrows my heart a little, it weighs on it.

Out of the shadows steps Mrs Reddan. Dallas is not happy to see her.

This is not God or person, but foulness. Mrs Reddan. How does she come here?

Mrs Reddan Perjurer, attacker, liar, murderer, you.

Thus say I, Mrs Reddan, out of Clare, that married Lucius Lysaght in his dotage.

I accuse you here, Dallas Sweetman, mere servant of the house, that you put death on my husband, first killing his hopes and then robbing his very wits.

That you, without a proper doubt, hurt his daughter, Lucinda, a woman you professed to love.

By first attacking her, and secondly, murdering her husband, Mountifort Longfield.

And most grievous to your soul, turned your coat, spitting on the old faith to take the new.

Dallas Sweetman, creeping, devious, darkened man. I accuse you.

Dallas This is not so. No murderer, I. I saw murder, but did not commit such crimes. How will I speak to it? I did not kill. I loved, and had no love returned, and served and wandered, but I did not kill.

(*Looking out.*) Are you then my judges? Not friend, not foe, but cold jurymen and women?

I have an accuser. Is there one appointed to defend me? Your silence tells me not. Then I must speak for myself, although, my little judges, you may say, how can we believe him?

And what have I in my defence?

A morsel, a story.

Only a story, and not even quite my own. For my life was lived in the shadow of another's, the person that I loved, Lucinda Lysaght, whom now I am accused of wronging with great evil.

Oh, hear me, hear me, so that my soul be not sucked down.

My one great love – I was nothing in her eyes. But she contained my reason to draw breath, to think the human thoughts of those that live, the daily half-discounted poetries of mere life. For her I lived and live, even in tasteless death.

And do long to see her.

Her ages and stations were curiously my own, and by her stations I measured my own life, and in their haunted mirrors I saw my looking face.

I loved her. Like a stag his mountain, the badger his muddy cave, the rabbit his own stupidity, the creeping fox his secret self, the robin his wife and ground, the wren his little size. Like a rook loves his storming tree, and ice seizes on the droplets of the rain and makes a cloth of snow, I loved her.

(*Loudly enough.*) Lucinda.

In this story is my defence, I know. I did and do not lie, I did not sully, I did not kill. As for coat-turning, I fear that is a strange, sad sport, in Ireland . . .

Some light now for Lucinda Lysaght.

Mrs Reddan Already he lies. He loved no one.

Now Lucinda appears.

And not this ruined girl. He gave her only madness.

Dallas Lucinda. Shining girl. But true Lucinda, or a shadow, or a thing of light? Can she hear me? See me?

Lucinda A wolf watching me, in the margin of the trees. It is a dark memory. Almost black. It was a great, grey, shaggy creature, and one paw snaked out on the damp grasses, where the sunlight was, itself quite civil and nice, and its red eyes stared into my own eyes. It was the first terror I remember. I could hear the wolf's heart beating, I thought, or else it was my own. The upper sky shrugged with thunder, like an enormous sleeper in a bed. I put out my hand to halt it, turning my palm to the creature; it is not a childish memory, but a woman's, a young woman's memory in the fire of the Irish summer.

And what can I, Lucinda Lysaght, bear witness to of happiness? Much, much. For I loved my brother Matthew, my very twin, and loved my father. My mother had been soon to go, but she left her light burning in the eyes of my father, like an afterglow in the evening sky above our hills. Most evenings we stood there in one especial place, beside our old stone house, my father, my brother and I, silent, watching the sun being quenched in the further ocean, beyond Sherkin Island and Cape Clear, and though we were silent, we knew he was thinking of her, my mother. It was our contentment.

At the heart of that contentment was a bud of fear.

As the sea and sky and the two islands trembled, I also trembled, a little girl in an embroidered dress, with a pattern of tiny roses, holding two hands, one large, one small as my own.

Perhaps even then the dark wolf lurked at the edge of all, in the black shadow of the Irish wilderness.

Dallas Now I am moved to truth. Her very presence warms my senses, and memory becomes all present moment. As I think, as I remember, I begin to see, and am there again.

I will strive to make you see.

My judges.

My story, my defence, my song of life, begins in Ireland, in an old stone house in the county of Cork, on the margins of the sea, just as she describes. I was servant to the Lysaghts, people of the old faith. Old English they were, not of the Gaelic lords, but pledged to withstand the floodwaters of Protestant desire. And loyal, loyal to a fault.

Lucinda's father was Lucius, my master.

Light now for Lucius, and the scene of the birth revealed. Lucius is near Dallas, at the 'door'.

Her mother, the famed Belinda, looked upon her twins only a few moments. Two perfect children she had carried into the world, for Lucinda was born in the same tumult with her brother Matthew.

I was the manservant hovering in the door, to be called and cursed at to fetch whatever women want for births – torn cloths and water, sugar sticks and beer.

I could see three candles in an ancient sconce. They threw down poor light on anguished features, the mother's eyes like something cooking in the kitchens, a sweat as cold as January floods rinsing her arms and breast.

In that far district we had but one beer-stewed crone, to be taking babies out.

In this instance, aided by the sister of Lucius.

Now the grubby midwife laboured over my mistress. Her arms were all windmills.

Lucius Sister, the child is delivered. Why still the straining?

Sister There is another baby hiding within.

Lucius Oh, my good Lord.

Sister We will have it out.

Lucius Oh, gently, gently, gently.

Dallas I saw in my mind's eye the cold figure of the sheelagh-na-gig, fastened to the church wall in the yard of the old house, as a warning to any girl who was carrying a babe to widen her human bones, or find death. For the child would be trapped in the mother, the mother trapped in the act of birth. A carved crone it was, roughly made with starved chest, the hands down at her opening, widening the lips.

That was our country medicine in that place.

In a deeper darker corner now, the crying boy was being wrapped, and warmed into delicate life, by his aunt, a woman who would later seek to be his murderer, in league with Mrs –

Mrs Reddan That is a lie. Oh, he speaks well enough. You are thinking, let us be friend to this man. Trust not in his speaking. The easy tone, the friendly tune. Judas was found hanging in the Potter's Field, for all his famous bonhomie.

Dallas The little girl appeared, coming out through the gate of life like a dancer, and was put on her mother for warmth.

The mother sang a whittled song to the storm-bird on her breast.

It was in the Irish tongue, for though she was Old English, they had spoke Irish also in their echoing rooms.

Belinda (*singing*) '*Seothín seo, ullaloo* . . . '

Lucius Ah, these are wonders worth witnessing, are they not, Dallas?

Dallas Yes, good master Lucius. (*To us.*) And Lucius stepped forward and touched the little fingers, marvelling at their size. He counted them, one by one. But beautiful Belinda Lysaght looked upon her daughter only a few moments.

She sang her honeyed song, and died.

Light away the scene.

(*After a little, to us.*) This man, Lucius Lysaght, was a little man, that is, in height. But in heart, his will was strong.

15

As I was his closest servant he often said, in secret in his room, that the Irish church must be spruced and rinsed.

The marriages of priests among the Gaelic chiefs enraged him.

Lucius Black scallywags –

Dallas – he called them.

He knew the history of Rome was poor. He thought our old local saint, with his box of salty bones in the seaside church, a curse, and a temptation to the superstitions of the poor. He had read old Erasmus and his treatise on Canterbury.

Lucius (*with a book now, close to Dallas*) Popes should not have armies, unless they are armies of prayers, nor seek to rule the temporal world.

And yet, whatever Pope sits there in Rome, is come down from Peter, and such is how things are, and we must strive for better. I cannot call a cankered, lusting King my All of All, nor such a king's daughter.

Dallas These things he whispered, and my ears were homes for all such things.

He and I together, master and servant, sequestered in private colloquy. Our faces looking such and such, nodding and honest.

He buried his wife with words so sweet and clear that foul beggars, waiting at the grave for the alms of grief, wept like children. Even such rubbed-out men felt the sorrow of the man, his mind so robed in Latin texts he spoke like a book.

Their thoughts were Gaelic and their curses too. But sorrow is in the pulsing of the words, it shows in the periods and spaces of speech. Those wretches wept.

And other princes of those far Cork lands, as fierce as Lucius to keep that Catholic world, looked drained of face, like slaughtered creatures hung up to bleed. And it was said, the beauty of his dame Belinda had disturbed the dreams of many another man in easier days.

Now, Belinda, for all her fame and vivid beauty, was no more, could not be ravished or wooed, but only mourned, and touched in sinful dreams.

She was buried. Now, a woman was required to raise the twins, and Mrs Reddan made her entrance.

And so she does – Mrs Reddan appears.

She was the kinswoman of my master and his sister, as thin as a half-seen spectre, and as malign.

She had the temperature of winter, and when I passed her in the hall, it was as if I had brushed against snow.

The sister it was who sent for Mrs Reddan. To what true end I did not immediately understand.

A chilling, dulling, heart-ruined creature was that woman.

Though in those first days, I must allow, she put herself faithful and fierce to her tasks. So much shitting, calling, crying and hunger there is in twins, a catastrophe of need.

Mrs Reddan holding the twins.

And Lucius saw that and trusted her.

Lucius appears.

Being a merchant in the main, he was bound to journey, and off he would go on missions to cajole and barter, in ports of Spain and Portugal. He burst through tempests, he carried wine and salt to Cork, then came the dusty, withering miles to Baltimore, where his mansion was, with two fine babies, and an empty bed.

It was easy to put his trust in what he did not know.

Lucius touches Mrs Reddan's hand a moment, and goes.

One terrible day, when he was far away, I saw a sight that frightens me to this day.

The Sister and Mrs Reddan have brought in a sort of framework, and are hanging the babies from it by their feet, so they are upside down.

The babes were about six months old, but they were not thriving. Both were measly, mewling, out of sorts. Wet nurse there being none just at that time, they were fed with good cow's milk, from our splendid herd. But whatever it was, the milk would not satisfy them. At first they often screamed and then, it seemed, submitted in some horrifying way, and merely cried like chicks. Lucius put his faith in Mrs Reddan that she could rectify them. Poor Lucius, innocent man.

I heard them, the sister and she, whispering in their room, and was not afraid to put my ear to the keyhole.

Mrs Reddan Your brother is trusting.

Sister Terrible ailments befall the young. He will not know.

Mrs Reddan We will do all carefully. Inch by inch, always watching behind. There are eyes not friendly to us, ears that would gather ill against us.

Sister Beware that creeping Dallas Sweetman, he is spy in chief.

Mrs Reddan A mere dog to be drowned.

Sister We can go around him. Furthermore, dear cousin, when the babes are gone, I will have everything after Lucius. And you will share in that.

Mrs Reddan Will you swear to that and sign it in a deed?

Sister I will write it in my blood.

Mrs Reddan Then I will do anything. The natural affection that we feel for these soft *leanbhs*, the sharp sting in the breast, must be put aside in this time of Irish tumult.

Dallas in desperation makes a stamping on the floor.

Hush, what is that? Take down these suffering babes.

They do so.

I read in a curious book that to invert a childish brain brings a storm of killing blood. Would it might do so more swiftly.

They each take a child.

We may continue to starve them, sup by sup. All must be natural, inconspicuous.

They see Dallas, and rock the babies in their arms.

Dallas Perhaps this promise of inheritance corrupted them, as it might a saint. Some parts of any history are dark, even to the teller. I do not know how it was, that Mrs Reddan, though kin to Lucius, had such a bile of evil in her.

Mrs Reddan Bile of evil. Easy it is to make me a puppet in his fairy tale. An old wives' tale of impossible cruelty. Anyone who believed him would be a staring fool. His course is a drunkard's, weaving and spilling and falling through the dark lanes of lies.

Dallas She was a good-faced woman but too small. Of course I never measured her, but if I could have stood near her, and dropped a cord from her crown, I think only some five brief feet would have been measured. And her arms were scant and loathsome I recall.

Mrs Reddan Oh!

She goes.

Dallas And she smelled of some foreign, fishy oil she liked to rub into her skin, which peeled off on the surface in the winter winds. Her husband, poor Mr Reddan, we were told, had died of terror, we knew not how. His heart had bursted.

She was to herself, I think, a kind of queen, imperial and chill. A Catholic woman with the disdain of ancient blood. Her mother's family were FitzGeralds, whose lands were forfeit and their chief men killed.

She in her own mind was quite so high that her crown touched Heaven daily. Her prayers went straight to God, her farts were perfume.

No farthing had she, no field, no house. It is a powerful cause.

Now, Lucius kept a simple world, a mere five hundred souls toiled in his fields. He had four hundred thousand acres, though mostly mountain and marsh. But even so, full twenty thousand acres groaned with wheat and beeves and barleys and the like. His merchant ways brought fortune also. And though he cursed his luck that kept him in Cork, the parliament never calling him, when he might have been a powerful governing man in Dublin, still he flourished.

All this knew Mrs Reddan.

And was by that inspired?

Music.

How those babes lived even a year gives evidence of their natural fortitude. Starving them, hanging them upside down no doubt, when I was not there to thwart it, everything short of sticking them with knives, did not destroy them. By the age of two, they were beginning to harvest language, and those two women feared them now as gradual witnesses to their miseries.

So – when these babes were about two years old, good Lucius went a-travelling. He was to be gone five weeks and more. Then to our story came added woe and woe, for the two women were like wolves in an element without humanity.

The old estate of Lucius took in the town of Baltimore, a little place, with Sherkin Island across a narrow bay, a few cold houses there.

And there was a strand that stretched for miles, all Lysaght land indeed, and quite deserted.

And so a favourite place for pirates, sun-darkened Arabs from North African shores, who liked to dip along the edge of countries, and take off people, that they might be slaves in Araby.

Every few years you heard the stories, girls in some seaboard farm took off by shadows, gaps made in families never filled. In greatest quiet, subtlety, and never an Arab seen, though some did say they saw a slinking ship put out past Sherkin on that boiling sea. And boys were sometimes took, and girls, and men and wives. And all to be put as slaves, to row, to toil, and worked till a last drop of physical element signalled death, unless those Christian souls were content to become Mohammedans, and put on new dresses in a marvellous land.

Mrs Reddan's measure of me had not improved.

Mrs Reddan pushing the twins along slowly in a basket on a 'pony', the blow of the sea, seabirds. She seems to be keeping a lookout for something.

Me she would not have near, though I was servant now *in officio* to the twins.

My task was to put order on their lovely clothes, to keep their ponies and their carriages ready, and in all manners to guard them, against robbers and religions.

Another man might have stood away and lazed, but I kept always near them.

I was like those Arabs, as a shadow, and when she was walking with them, I crept along behind, and when she was talking to them, or barking or hissing sternly, I listened at the doors for fear of further harm. I bustled in at mealtimes, having seen what I saw, and she and her cousin were forced to give them food, while I lingered by.

Strange things I noted. She had some tenderness of heart, in that if a child got an injury that she had not schemed, she petted and patted it. But she had no knowledge of children's games or joy, as if she had travelled from a childless country, where such things were not known.

But, being a watchful man, thus it was I saw what she did that day.

It was a day of blowing sunshine, in the summer early, the beginning of sailing weather, that brought away merchants and brought merchants in.

A swelling up of the scene behind.

You would think in those recent weeks that the old strand was the special love of Mrs Reddan, for every day she brought the twins there alone, and walked austerely on the long shore path, the children bobbing in a basket on a moorland pony, a thing they loved above all else.

I heard them laughing as was their way.

I made sure to stay unseen, creeping along if needs must through briary hedges and the like.

Then that sight I saw: Mrs Reddan stopped.

All as he describes, as if it were the theatre of Dallas's inner eye.

There was a distant boat out on the water, with stooping sails, and I saw her view it.

Even the back of her hatted head had cold intent.

Whether she planned what followed I do not know. Had she made pact with barbarous men, those very men of Barbary itself, by some system of messages or communication?

She glanced all about, then turned again towards the sea – did she hesitate? – and went with the pony halfway down the strand.

Mrs Reddan puts the nosebag on the creature, and hobbles the back legs, and tucks the babes down firmer in their basket, as if with a mother's wish to see them warm.

Mrs Reddan (*cupping her hands, blowing into them, so that she makes a noise like a hooting owl*) Hoo, hoo!

Dallas Then she looked about again, went down to the waves and strongly called, and called, hallooing like that witch the peasants say announce a family death, the foul banshee.

She tends to the babies one last time, kisses her right hand and touches each baby with the hand.

Then gaining the path again, she walked away.

I stood in my covered place and wondered.

I could not immediately understand.

Mrs Reddan turned an angle of the beach and disappeared. I was fearful and puzzled.

Out from the side of the distant boat pushed a smaller craft, and against the surfy waves began to row.

Music. The pirates a presence in their black clothes.

In my horror I fancied I saw in the breeze hooded vestments blowing like slack sails.

I burst out of my cover and hared along the strand.

Hardly thinking of any plan, I unharnessed the children who with childish words greeted my coming as a thing of ordinary joy.

Then I stuck one under each arm and left pony and basket to their fates, and struggled back up the sand, hoping that no one saw.

My chief thought was them, and Lucius too. I sensed the danger all around. The approaching pirates and Mrs Reddan's evil wish.

It would be two weeks before he returned, two dangerous, unknown weeks. She might do a worse thing. She might quickly banish me, and have the babes to her own devising.

Her mighty word against my own!

Once she had gone this far, she would have no further stop, unless I could outwit her.

Now the pirates fading.

I carried the babies back.

Two-year-old babies are not feathers. They seem light at first, but step by step they gain in weight, till a man must be groaning.

The colours of trees and undergrowth, the dark of a daylight wood. Music.

But I scarcely felt it. I plunged into the ancient woods of oak and beech, a hundred acres they covered, against the winter storms. I snaked my way on through, under the gloom of the trees I planned my plan.

The light clearing.

At length I was at the old middens of the house. There was a little door, which the scraps-man used, and unlike the rest of the castle few went that way.

I climbed up and up the mansion to the highest floor.

That realm of serving maids was quiet in the day. I went further by a doorway that I knew, that could bring the carpenters and the slaters to the roof, whenever the rain came in.

It was a town of attics. And in the deepest room, I set down the children – I must allow on the edge of fear, their eyes close to crying. But I let them bump about, and made it as a game, and soon they were not even glancing at me, but played as they used with intent and calm.

Do not ask me how luck stayed with me. I went back down into the house and ransacked an unused room. I brought a poor maid's bed upstairs and some goosedown peltings that I found. Then I made fast their door and crept down into the proper house to see what was afoot.

Mrs Reddan walking about in distress.

Mrs Reddan Oh, God, that I might undo this serious day. That I might drive back the sun into its bed from which it rose this morning, that I might put dark again upon the sea, and place back the little birds in their secret nests, and still the dawn wind, unwind it backward, make time regret its coming and go back!

Dallas Mrs Reddan had raised the house. She was still there herself, calling and crying, issuing order upon order. I asked a fellow servant what was what. (*To a passing woman.*) You there, Johanna, what passes here?

Servant Mrs Reddan was set upon as she walked on the strand. The babes have been taken by dark evil men. She herself is lucky to be alive. She has shown us all her scratches and shed blood.

Dallas (*aside*) I knew in my soul she had done all that with briars.

Servant This is a tragic day, and the master away on his journey. What horrible news will await him, unless we can rescue those babes.

Dallas Men were sent down to the sea and found the poor pony and its empty creel. No sign of those pirates on the leaping sea. No sign of the babes of Lucius. A terrible hue and cry.

At the centre of all, Mrs Reddan, and a mill of activity around her, again like a dance.

Now men were sent careening out on horseback to search the ways about.

Mrs Reddan wept and tore her hair like a Grecian tragedian. All was utmost pandemonium, concatenation, and loudest of all her selving blame –

Mrs Reddan I am the guilty one. Why did I not fight harder? Why did I shrink back in cowardly weakness? Oh, that I were wolf or man, not woman, weak and slight. My tender charges, two souls the same as life, my nesting birds, emblems of goodness, softness, love. Now Lucius will have me killed and well deserved. Oh, well deserved.

She is comforted by her cousin and others.

Dallas And on that occasion, the serving girls were allowed to comfort her.

Sister You are lucky to be alive yourself, good Mrs Reddan. You must have fought like a demoness.

Dallas Like a demoness was right.

My thoughts were all Lucius. Let him just return. Let them think what they wanted for the nonce, it made no odds. Indeed, said I to myself, let the rumour of this thing penetrate to whatever region he now traversed.

I fed the babes by childish morsels carefully fetched. Ten times in the day I checked them, and chased them about, playing that Monster game they loved.

I bedded them in at night, then locked the door. They were too small to question and faithfully filled their pots with piss and such, which I ferried down to the midden like a mouse.

I kept all a secret and shared my fear with none.

Then Lucius's return was nearer, near. Then he was home.

Lucius returning in his travelling coat. The household to meet him.

Oh, fearful scene. Yet I could not say my tale. Not for the moment.

In the old hall stood Lucius, draped in dust, listening to Mrs Reddan with her hanging face. He listened and in his goodness made no sound.

Mrs Reddan Dear Lucius, dear cousin closer to me than my heart. How can I say the hurting words? – The two babes are gone. Taken by pirates.

Dallas Did his sorrowing mind for a moment think, now this cold streak of womanhood is my heir? I do not know. Her own dark mind must have, of course.

*Mrs Reddan falls to her knees and grips the legs of
Lucius.*

Mrs Reddan I proffer my neck for death – let me be
killed. Draw out your sword, and lift it high, and strike
me with it. Let me not have mercy. Lucius, Lucius,
murder me. It will be better than living with this
murderous hurt and guilt.

After a moment, Lucius stoops and helps her rise.

Lucius stepped one step forward and held her arm.
Gently he held it. I slipped away.

Night came. I bided my time.

*He picks up the babies again. An enormous redness
everywhere.*

I sat with my little ones under the roof. It was that fierce
twilight of the west when somewhere in the ruckus of the
world the sun plunges down.

Then I took my charges, under each arm as before, and
stole down though the grieving house.

I left by the midden door and out into the oaks I went,
like a very thief myself.

Then by another path I came to the great frontals of the
house, and calling out, I cried my joyful news! *The
children are safe*, I called. *The children are safe. Rejoice.*
O springing joy. Great commotion in the hall. Lucius
fetched.

Lucius comes and takes the children into his arms.

Lucius Dallas, my servant, do you bring ghosts, do you
bring spectres from my own aching dreams?

Dallas No, my master, living hearts.

(*To us.*) Such reckless tears and commendations and wild questions.

Lucius How could it be? How are the babes not harmed, or starved?

Dallas I do not know. I made one last pilgrimage to the wastes, by what instinct or prompting is unknown. And there I found, miraculously, the lost babes. They were lying in a nest of heather, neat and plump.

Lucius Look, look, Mrs Reddan, it has all come good. Some great action of God has brought them home, unharmed.

Mrs Reddan's face.

Oh, even in my acting, how I loved to see her face, the utter bewilderment that could look like the edge of joy.

Mrs Reddan forces a smile, then utters a series of strange little shouts, then kisses the babies.

My babes, laughing and smiling at these festive acts.

What could she say?

Mrs Reddan This is mystery. I wrestled with those pirates till the blood spurted from my arms. They tore them from my grip. They knocked me down. I saw them row away on the enamelled sea. It is so clear in my mind. How are they saved? I do not know, I do not know, but, praise God, praise God!

Lucius This is a welcome and clear act of God. He looks down upon us and sees our pulsing need. He viewed me as a grieving father, whose own mere heart was breaking in the dark, whose bag of prayers was emptied, close to whose lips were curses against that God, may God forgive my lack of faith.

Dallas Such did their infant peril pass.

Now, Mrs Reddan more alone, as if a friend to us.

Mrs Reddan Now I must talk to this.

Please witness my solemn words.

When I was a young girl I walked out of Belmullet to marry a man in Sligo. I went with a little retinue of my father's servants, hoping not to be devoured on the way, because in that time there were always banditti lining the ways. I was very excited to be going to see my husband. He was the son of the Lord of Inniscrone, a very fine and civilised family. Of course there was not any real roads, our guides had just inklings and 'I think it might be this way' to go by. That was the way of things. We might have sailed from Belmullet to Sligo, except it was early spring, and the sea was just a great acreage of barns and castles – that is, those dark Atlantic waves.

As we went up by Ballina under the mountains called there Nephin, my husband's people came out to meet us, and guarded us all the way then to his door, with tremendous noise and colloquy.

We were married for ten years before a depredating army of Elizabeth our Queen was sent into Connaught to harass my husband, leading to his terrible defeat under the mountain of Knocknarea. My husband, though exhausted from a long defence, would not yield on any ground, knowing full well all his lands were at stake, and his history in that fabled place, and died of a bursted heart. So I was obliged then to seek refuge with my cousin Lucius, who graciously and with the kindness of family, took me in. But this was a ferocious plummeting down from those heights I had attained. Yet I was grateful for that mercy.

For many years then I attended to his children and sought to nourish them, knowing that a family thrives only by the progress of its progeny.

I say all this to show you, I am a woman of good family. I am accused of treachery greater than any I have ever heard of. To work against the children of my husband. Not plausible, not possible, as in an old story, and not true.

They disappeared it is true for some weeks, stolen I thought from the beach, and indeed I was in a fervour of despair. I saw no pirates, nor wrestled with them. It was shadows and monsters in Dallas Sweetman's mind, or a great invention. I had never thought to harm them, only mourned their loss, and was overjoyed when he magicked their return. And why he thought to work that trick on me I do not know.

Dallas Mrs Reddan having met this check on her plans, seemed to quieten in her malice, though persisted in her rationing of the children's food, and kept them lean and crying.

Mrs Reddan Lies are breeding lies, mother mouse brings forth her babies, it is most terrible.

Dallas But Lucius in his lovely thanks became more watchful of them, and maybe loved them better, and indeed made me protector of them in his own mind, and called me The Man of Miracles.

Music, a few moments.

Since I had scraps of Latin, and knew the history of the world, having once myself been well-to-do, but fallen now – my father had lost his portion at the tables of Dublin in a forgotten youth, and left us only with puzzles, hanging himself one Sunday morning from the yardarm of a wreck on Dollymount strand – since these things were so, Lucius chose me to school the children, and so I did.

My faith was fine as his, though faith without a fortune can be dim. I imparted to them the Romish things we loved, the why and wherefore, and the dark sins of those that had followed a lusting King, in their arrogance and with oppressing deeds.

I showed them the church in Baltimore out of whose yards we Catholics had been driven, though it was our own, with condemnations.

How Lucinda beat her fists together, raging at my histories.

Taught them to love their father, and to give thanks they had such wealth even history could not alter the altitude of the Lysaghts.

And I taught them to count on fingers, and to sing, and country dances that they might dance, when they were grown, at Catholic gatherings of Old English types, where they might find husband for one and wife for the other.

   Music. Now two young children dance.

(*After a little.*) And moment by moment, day by day, I grew to love them, and looked at all things that moved towards them with a fierce suspicion, and searched out all happenings for hidden violence, though I was in certain ways a stranger in Ireland – but a stranger, a mere Sassanach as the peasants say, may have love as deep as any.

Years went by – long years for them, as the years to children seem, a too-brief term to me. Terrible wars engulfed the old realms of Munster.

On the better lands, old lords and lordlings were murdered quite away, new English armies crushed Old English hopes.

But still the Lysaghts on the margins held.

Then, in those civil evils, wide as the State, befell another, a smaller matter none the less of greater evil. It happened to Lucinda.

Lucinda The wolf in the shadows. I was just a young woman, about fourteen. Many women of that age married in Ireland, but I was pledged to no one.

This memory mingles with Dallas Sweetman, he swirls about there, like dark berryjuice dropped in water.

Dallas Sweetman. He seemed to me immaculate and strange. He had taught me everything he knew of facts and figures and wonders, of stars and the sun, of the Greeks and of the Carthaginians, of Romans, their poetries and their gods. His words fell into my childish lap like coins, all the riches of his mind minted into words that came solid into my self, like a soft intrusion. I dreamed of him at night and even by day he seemed more dream than something truly real. I clothed him about with girlish light.

Mrs Reddan Then a dark year came, and there passed a story that grieves me still to say.

And I could never be certain of that story, to speak to Lucius, but certain enough to doubt and fear his servant.

One morning early in the late of summer, when the year begins to turn to thoughts of death, going up with water and apples to Lucinda, I found her bed empty. There was a terrible fear in me, and dark certainty of some harm. I went out into the meadows and moved through bulking cows, and over to the path that took me to the woods, and into the dripping, darkening trees, and by some rich instinct of kinship and love, following an ancient path, soon into a glade I came, the first cold sunlight roofing it, and there in the centre in the weakening grass, I saw her, wounded and cold herself, not asleep but weeping. Had someone fetched her from her very bed, covered her head in cloths, and stolen her away, to harm and enfold her in that place? She would never say. I took the hood from her head, and held her, but could not get her to speak for days. And the only hint of her trouble was, she could not be near to her erstwhile servant Sweetman, but kept away from him, trembling and sad. So I suspected him.

Lucius put out a notice of words that anyone found to have effected this crime would be, according to old laws, castrated, and his limbs lopped off, his entrails dragged steaming from his belly and fed before him to pigs, and then be dragged into the roughest field, and dragged about drearily, and hung until dead, and quartered, into four quarters like a very Ireland.

Dallas God above all gods! What happened is not known. Lucinda never spoke. Lucius suspected that out from those woods came a creeping wolf, a cold brute, one of those new men of England as may be. Perhaps such a man thought Ireland was just wildernesses, uncivil, and everything there was for him to take, to seize.

Yes, Mrs Reddan found Lucinda calling, bleeding in a larksome dell, the birds of the summer innocently singing all about. She gathered her up, and carried her into the house, just as I had when she was a little one, and helped her to her chamber, and drew water for her from the kitchens. And Lucinda asked that I not be called, I know, but for a reason I could not fathom. Oh, this I swear, before the courts of God, before you, my judges, this I swear, without fear of Hell for so terrible a lie.

For it is simple truth.

Mrs Reddan This is his bleakest lie, that he saw her in terms of love, and did not molest her innocent self. I suspect him, I suspect him.

Dallas Let me go on, as best I can, my self diminished by those accusations.

Ireland herself diminished, the country seemed to narrow. Lucius's old trade of hides and tallow, sent forth upon the earth for wines and salt, was faltering. The very old faith on which he rested was proving his undoing.

But not yet, not yet.

He feared everything. He feared of course for his daughter now the most, for her further destruction. He feared to send his son to Dublin, as his family had been wont, for dread of some Protestant discussion that might foul his mind. So he resolved to send them out to Lisbon, where by long trade and courtesy he knew the royal house, and especially that lady called the Princess of Brazil, a deep, shining, Catholic woman. And there his son Matthew might learn the laws of man and God, and Lucinda be made safe in the refuge of a royal court.

And she the great princess was anxious so to have them, for fear some Protestant might seek Lucinda's hand. She was not told I am sure of Lucinda's ordeal, in case it would place a mark of spoliation on her, in the manner of the time.

She was fourteen now, and by the grave of my father, I do swear, never had I seen so beautiful a girl.

The vision of Lucinda in her beauty.

I was thirty years old, yet she pulled my heart.

Soft and trim, no painter would need to dissemble her in the painting, she had no blemish that I could see, and had a brilliant, forceful, seeing, asking mind.

She had stretched my knowledge to the furthest reach. I had described to her in desperation the very waterfalls at the edge of the known world, though in truth I had not seen them.

And I prayed in my secret mind that something might
happen in my uncertain world to restore me to fortune,
so I could ask for her – though I sensed it a foolish
prayer. Yet the country was tumbling all about, who
would say where things might rest.

But Lucius feared that Irish world as much as loved.
Great lords had been dissolved like uncertain snows in
April.

Old companies of servants, old households, with
stewardships and the like going back five hundred years,
had proved not great woods but drifts of snowdrops.

The gears of religion were grinding, impatient winds were
blowing across the land, new English hearts beat loudly
for Irish land. And we had seen possible evidence of their
rapine, their careless hatred of us, and their mocking
force. New English rapining Old English, ugly tune!

And though great Elizabeth loved Old English lords, she
said, for being ever true to her crown, yet now, Lucius
saw, there was a new voice in her throat. And her agents
were men of death. And he feared that his babes might
be engulfed, or their souls robbed away by that swelling
faith he feared, as well as their very forms.

At fourteen packed away to Lisbon!

Lamentation in that Lysaght house, the very last blooms,
the very last roses pulled from out the ground.

But Lucius was sure.

Lucius embraces his children.

I was not sent with them. He went the way himself and
returned alone, and I suspected why.

That Lucius had watched me with her, and knew my
heart.

Lucinda Bound for Lisbon. To leave my father.

But something of me was a ghost, left behind in Ireland.
A dream afflicted me, over and over, even in the huge
richness of a royal palace. Myself alone, on the wet grass.
The eyes of the wolf shining in the dark like emeralds
no one would want. In my throat was trapped the word,
'Dallas', that I wanted to shout out, for the rescue of his
love. But no one came, eternally.

The dream, the dream. But is it a dream? I am always
there, standing by the wood.

The upper sky shrugging with thunder, like an enormous
sleeper in a bed.

And then, like a storm finally breaking, the grey figure
breaks from the trees. Running at me in leaping arcs,
smoking with hair, and mangy, terrible, it reaches me,
and as it does, the word breaks at last from my mouth,
'Dallas, Dallas.'

And the wolf devours me.

And the wolf is only a man, a man of ordinary evil, that
tries to rob the soul out of me, but he fails.

But he fails while I tense in awful terror.

No terror ever again like to it.

Fear so deep the devil in Hell is aware of it.

And the man searches about in my person, tearing and
destroying, and when he seems to find what he sought,
leaves me.

I lie in a stupor of hurt and despair.

Deeply ashamed, shame as deep as the devil in his burning
lair.

Who comes? It seems to be no one, a person of shadow, with ragged wings, like an angel of the old faith, but it digs its arms under me, and lifts me, and carries me across the lawn, my blood falling on the grasses, and into the house.

That I think must have been Mrs Reddan, in other instances not a true friend to me.

Perhaps my enemy.

In that instance, almost a mother.

Mrs Reddan's face, listening, alert.

And later, when I slept and woke, I told her about the wolf. And she told me the wolf was caught, and hung like a pig, its throat cut, and its blood gathered in a bucket to make night charms, in the dark of my father's granary.

And I was no longer a child from that day.

And I asked her not to bring Dallas to me, because I was ashamed.

I thought he would detest me now, because of the great calamity of my pollution, and would see me as beautiful no longer, because I did believe he thought me so, though he never said a word, nor ever spoke to me except as a loving servant.

My father's loving servant.

My first beloved.

That did destroy me after.

Then when my father said he would send me to Lisbon, I allowed it, almost gladly, thinking it would serve me in Dallas's love, and save him from bearing such grievous news, or to suffer the sight of me.

On the cold ship that ducked round the old toes of Ireland, I wept. My brother Matthew sat by my side. I wept. I had lost my world. The softness that moved over my father's face when he looked at me. The way he would sometimes count my fingers, as he spoke to me, idly, finger by finger, as if by that action he might recover paradise.

Music.

Act Two

As before.

Mrs Reddan Now, where stand we, as the old ballad says? You have heard his tricky whistle-tunes, how he works to convince you with matters a credulous child would baulk at. He took to the great river so confidently in his little boat of truth. He has glided softly between the leafy banks, the sun has been kindly on his shoulders. But now the river widens and in the distance is the scuffy vapour of the falls, and the first faint hint of its roaring.

Dallas Then were there years of many-headed woe. No Lucinda, the old skies of Ireland without their sun, and the country ravished.

Ambitious, Protestant generals wished for those Lysaght lands.

We journeyed, Lucius and I, and a small company, to London to speak to the Queen.

He was speaking for all the loyal princes of the south and west, and other points.

The glimmering faint figure of Elizabeth in her majesty.

Lucius That we may sue to thee, Majesty, and ask for the great comfort of thy bosom, turned towards Ireland, that you might feed your kith and kin and faithful hearts, and be the great mother that thou art, and not forsake us as Fate rises to confound us.

Elizabeth Good Sir Lucius, rest your mind. We are not a woman to forsake that Ireland, lying in the dark waters of the Atlantic like a drowning girl. We will give thee our gentling word and affectionate phrase, to carry back to the home place, where we will guard thee with our good will and special grace, and never be aught but protector to Ireland.

Lucius Gracious and perfect Majesty, I hope my poor and rusted English, so long lying out in the rains of Ireland, will convey to you my love and permanent loyalty.

Elizabeth Even as your loyalty, also our love. For I would send blessings unto Ireland, I would send a portion of our English sunlight, I would send unto Ireland the benefice of our beautiful Englishness, perfecting, quietening, finishing Englishness. Or else with hard hammer, heavy sword, vicious arrow and thundering gun, I would send into Ireland want, pestilence, narrowness, hunger and Death.

Lucius (*on one knee*) My gracious Queen.

Dallas All that was wonders. Her paper features, her strange darkness peeping through the white, her dress of gold stars and firing silver rods, the very seep and rancour of her court, the tides of knowledge and shoaling talk.

Lucius saw the Raleghs and the Earls she loved, and noted, like the scholar that he was, how his own English was astray from hers, her talking odder, quicker, deeper than his own, as if that English brought to Cork five hundred years before had grown different, and was almost two differing tongues.

But not two hearts. His own heart, he avowed, beat with a killing love for her, her might, her history, and her chilling eye.

To the play that night. It was a new-made one, called *As You Like It*, and a wondrous thing all of itself.

I had not seen any play before, being a confined and rural man.

But this was a play of metal, yet light as air, and everyone there did love that Rosalind, and for me she was my Lucinda, all grown and fierce and kind, and I wondered as I watched what was befalling her in Lisbon.

And the author himself played an old man, and was wellnigh devoured with shouting at the end, with praise and love. And we laughed at poor Jaques for his saddened talk and his bleak speech of the Seven Ages, now so well known, but then played for the first time, so that it fell on us like a miracle. And we universally desired only to lie an hour with Rosalind, though the part be played of course by a pretty boy.

And for myself, that night, I dreamed it seemed to me a new dream of Lucinda, new and unchanged. The play released in me a possibility, that when she returned, it might be for me. And in the strange dream I dreamed a marriage.

Lucinda lying asleep and Dallas in his dream approaches and stoops to her and takes her in his arms.

Then at the wish of Lucius we went down by the fabled road to Canterbury, to shrive ourselves of sins, marvelling at that pretty country, taking a sup at a creaking inn, and strode in together to that tremendous place, all pillars reaching to a perfect heaven, stars in the roof, and a vastness of half-light and ancient prayers. And Lucius knelt in his deep Catholic way at the very spot where once St Thomas had been, in his hut of gold and jewels, and prayed near that absence and to that absence, in abject and wonderful faith.

There in the gloom, like a quaint and Irish Erasmus, in the curious light of ancient stone, a light that has played lover to darkness, he told me a story – not an ancient story, but an old one, something from his father's generation. It meant the world to him that I should hear his story, but to me it seemed only a tale of shadows and ghosts. For I was young.

Lucius It was here, Dallas, when old King Henry was young, about the year 1540, in the time of our fathers, in his efforts to dismantle our old faith, that he ordered St Thomas Becket be called from his tomb to answer to charges of treason and heresy, and if he did not answer the call, that he be tried in his absence. For Henry loved nothing better than to be lawful in all things, even in his unlawfulness. The thought of his ancestor, old Henry II, being obliged, after Thomas was murdered, to come in through Canterbury on his knees, and reaching the altar, to strip himself bare, and be beaten by the monks with whips, to expiate his guilt in the murder, incensed our later Henry, as if it had been the work of the last week. They stood here, the officials, right on this spot, and cried out for Thomas Becket to attend them. They stood on the altar, looking up the long reaches of the cathedral, the tomb just visible in the distance. 'Come down, Thomas Becket,' shouted they, 'Come down.' For a moment one of them thought they saw a stir of light, and a great fear seized them that the choleric saint was coming. For he was well known in his lifetime for his beautiful anger.

But of course he had been lying in his tomb three hundred years and more . . . They waited the thirty days and, St Thomas not complying, they tried him in the Archbishop's palace in Lambeth, the King supplying a good advocate to defend our saint. And, in due course, it was found he had been traitor to his king, and heretical to his own church. And that he was henceforth to be known not as a saint, but to be called merely Bishop Becket, his name and image to be erased from windows and rubbed out of old books, his bones to be taken from his tomb, and crisply burned, and thrown to the four winds, and his tomb to be destroyed and carried away. And all veneration, exhortation and pilgrimage in his name to cease. And in just a few years, Henry effected his great sundering of men's belief, parting and altering Christ's old river, decreeing two channels, and made one poison to the other, which plagues us to this day, oh most especially in Ireland. Where there was surely sundering enough without that.

Henry II, by speaking in anger about Becket before his knights, may have seemed to commission his murder, but he went into Ireland also later, to expiate that seeming sin, at the request of the Pope, to reform the Irish church, even then showing pustules and cankers on its face. So if this spot be sacred on account of St Thomas, so is it also on account of that Henry, who knelt here in his pelt, because it was he brought us Old English first into Ireland. And so Lysaghts have always come on pilgrimage to Canterbury, if in these days more discreetly, and I hope always will.

Dallas That is a curious old tale, my master.

Lucius But true. Perhaps all souls might be called to account in this place. Why not? There is a myriad of things unknown.

Dallas And having said all that, home we hied to our vexed island.

Then, by our ironical history of Ireland, Lucius was forced out to war, Great Elizabeth not having such great control of her ravening generals as we had hoped, or indeed as she had promised. And in that shift of things we sensed even greater darkness coming.

It was a new English lord that took it in his head that all Old English lords were weakened.

And fell upon Lysaght lands with his teeming army.

Now that great mildewed, massive, unwashed army was composed of savage men, the like of demons in an ancient story. They spoke their different English like a pouring sewer. It was rasping, grinding, crashing in the mouth, with their howling phrases, and their spitting wit. They seemed to know not *civis*, *civitas* or *urbs*, though they fought in the name of Elizabeth.

Such fell on Lucius Lysaght.

We geared ourselves to fight.

Since I was a servant I but followed Lucius to war. Yet I hoped it might bring me my change of fortune.

Now Lucius in his battle gear.

I had no honoured place, but banged his gear and plates back smooth like a blacksmith in the evening, and combed his hair, and picked the white lice off his vests and pants – (*doing so*) – because at war there was no washing, and those English hordes were lousy as a ship.

The battle – the new English lords and their men against Lucius and his men. Slow killing and toil. Music.

That was the battle of Baltimore, if you have heard – long piles of killed swordsmen, with lacerated limbs, and so much blood, we called the field the Field of Blood from that time on.

Picture the beautiful army of Lucius, in their honoured suits, a hundred men of substance from his lands. Picture the opposing rabble that stood for an army, in their thirsting, hungry manner. Hear the harsh, roaring leader floundering on, and steel entering those extraordinary breasts, as brave as bears must be, and elegant in some wise as wolves.

How we managed to crush them, I do not know. The old Christian God smiling not upon the new.

But even in general victory, my own heart was mired in bitter thoughts.

No moment came, no chance of valour, or work of victory proper to myself.

Onlooker only ever, debased, crushed down by my unlucky father, I returned to our mansion only the servant I was, unchanged.

Mrs Reddan I took their coming strangely. I did not like to see that man return, that Dallas Sweetman, with his lying name. I knew my lovely Lucinda was safe from him in Lisbon, and was grown a woman too, but still, to see that thieving ignorant soul return, even though it brought Lucius home – I could not be glad.

Oh, let me present a comely history, concordant with the facts.

By this time, though Lucius was growing old, we had wed. I was content to be the human coals to warm his side. I loved him, and he loved me, and his sister loved me, and she knew I would not upset her portion. I bore a child to him, late though I was in the summer of my life. Lucius called me beautiful, though I was not, God knew, and yet in my confinement he prayed at the door, for the mercy of a deliverance. God heard his excellent prayers. He was a caring, curious, contenting man.

Dark looks and hatred was all I got from Dallas Sweetman, and at my request he was put out on the land, to work as a steward, and not set his boots indoors, though in truth he was for ever creeping in. His hopeless performance at the war, proving himself a mere servant in his soul, had also altered him in Lucius's sight, who had expected better of him. Now he was not a man of miracles, but of falling.

This is better truth.

Lucinda and Matthew had been sent to Lisbon, yes. After some years of study, Matthew went ever deeper in his fervent prayers, and became a monk.

But Lucinda could not abide where she was. Her simple loving heart always turned to Lucius, her own heart calling to his heart across the sea between them. And we feared her return, Lucius and I, for her sake.

There was nothing of Dallas Sweetman in it, he was quite forgotten in her heart.

Burned away, a dry leaf in a bonefire.

Dallas How like that ruined, ended, blinded, scrap of Jaques's I am, here in this place of darkening fortune, telling of things long past, as if to tell them were to live them o'er again.

Dust in my mouth the meat of other days, dust in my crown the blowing summer days.

When youth was there but not accounted, youth was there and never noticed.

And nothing built up as ballast against this factual struggle of old age.

But I must go on, recount to you this most grievous passage coming, when things so happened that I lost my better soul.

Sweet judges, listen, and understand me, as I paw at the four locked gates of the New Jerusalem, ever locked against me.

Music.

A fellow like me come out of England on his father's side, and whose mother moreover was a Godkin from the Barony Forth of Wexford, still may love Ireland.

But Ireland changes by the year, she is like the barnacle that becomes the goose at length, and who could tell their cousinage?

Yet for a truer native like Lucinda, Ireland is a tune, a ground of life, a telling story.

And she wrote to tell Lucius she was sorry homesick for us all, for him in chief (I hoped a touch for me).

Lucinda (*reading the letter*) 'My beloved father, loved above all others.

'While well understanding the reasons for my exile, I am sending this to you as an opening of my heart.

'My father, I yearn to lay my head on your shoulder as in our old days, and sit with you as we once did, and go out into the failing light and see the sun go down in all his kingly attire, red and gold, and stand together in the old silence.

'The fields, the meadows, the margins of woods, the islands beyond – all call me home. The edifice of what you are, most of all.

'My father, allow me to come home, if only for a stated term. I am withering here in Lisbon, despite the great kindness of the Princess, and all the promise of what I will inherit. Spread of orchards, infinite estates, are very little beside my love for you.

'Your daughter, Lucinda.'

Lucius with the letter, Dallas attending.

Lucius I tell you, this must be done well. Now even more than before the Protestant heresy looms over young minds. I would she might stay in Lisbon. But if home she must come, it will be by strict instructions. She must travel with a trusted priest and speak to no one, unless they are vouched for by religion and name. I will write to her, Dallas, and say these things.

Dallas That is wisdom, sir, doubtless.

And so he did.

The Princess of Brazil comes forward, Lucinda before her. The Princess is very gorgeous and wonderful in her clothes. She lifts a crucifix and advances on Lucinda, as if to drive it through her head. Lucinda doesn't flinch.

And the Princess of Brazil was of the same mind as Lucius.

Princess I beg thee, little waif and wanderer, not to travel to so benighted and disastrous a country, where my own influence is a sparrow's. Stay with me here, marry a person of this court, and I will grant thee lands and title, and make thee a proper Portuguese lady, and shrive all Irishness from you, as a token to pull thee from Death both temporal and spiritual.

Lucinda My heart aches for Ireland, Majesty, and for the embrace of my father.

Princess But I have such orchards and acres to give, stay with me here, do not risk to go back into that foul country, once so sweet with Catholic thought, but now like a poisoned well, that may kill you to drink from.

Lucinda (*opening her palms in supplication*) Let me go, great Princess, back into the embrace of my father and my country.

Dallas So, a priest was chosen of immaculate character, that he might protect her, a man of darkened middling years.

She travelled with this man in some small splendour, in that she had always near her a gold toilet equipage so she might keep herself dainty on the journey, to the value of five thousand pounds.

If she married of course, she was to bring an enormous dowry to that man, as being the only girl, and dearly loved and prized by her father, all the more so now her brother was a monk.

Whoever wed her would take the Lysaght name unto himself, and be a sort of semi-Lysaght for the ages.

I do not know the weather for her ship, but it duly brought her to Rosscarbery, in her own county of Cork.

The sound of harbour water and the bells and knockings of ships. Lucinda in her travelling cloak.

In the small hours of the night it docked.

When first light came she gathered her dresses and herself, and her equipage was to be following after.

The gangplank, by a forced provision of the tide, had quite a span between ship and shore. As she crossed over, her dresses caught in something, and pulled her sideways, and she fell with a yelling splash into the filthy harbour, causing the sailors and the captains there to scurry about like woodlice disturbed by a lifted rock.

Lucinda simply sits on the ground, the cloak spreading as if floating.

The priest in whose care she was, hesitated and dithered, not knowing what to do, and fearing the water himself.

Her dresses held her floating. But slowly, down between the terrible ship and the stony harbour wall, she could be seen to be sinking, sinking.

Suddenly from out the idle crowd a man came forth.

He was a tall, dark-suited man, with a beaky nose, and he jumped quite fearless into the brine, and came up just beside her, and catching a rope thrown down, pulled her to him like the wisp she was, and bound the rope around her, and the sailors pulled her up, then threw it for him again.

The Reverend Mountifort Longfield appears, ties a rope around her.

Lucinda stood pouring on the dockside, but refusing to move away, still peering back down at her rescuer.

In the slug of the tide, the ship pressed closer to the wharf, pinning the gentleman below. With keenest thought, she arranged the sailors on the stones, and told them to push at their gigantic ship, and rock it by inches back, and this they did, and the unknown man was free, and was pulled up.

When he came to the top of the wharf, dripping and laughing, with a broken hand, Lucinda fell to her knees and thanked him, and gazed up at the face that had given her back her life.

Mountifort pulls her close.

It was a long, strange face, but laughing still, and it was then the poor priest saw that the man was a reverend of that very selfsame creed she was to have been protected from.

She saw this too, but seemed to have no pain of it.

She looked at the fuddled priest, and this easy, smiling man, and maybe in that moment she made a choice, and suffered some dark sea-change.

At any rate, news came to us in Baltimore that she was betrothed to be wed.

Lucius appears.

To this very man –

Lucius This evil minister –

Dallas – as Lucius called him, as he paced his private rooms. The priest himself carried this terrible news.

He was not just raging, poor Lucius Lysaght, but also weeping. He boiled up against this unknown man, this thief of his daughter. He wished him dead, he wished him gone.

Lucius That my own sweet child should bring this catastrophe on me. To a family that for five hundred years has worshipped at a proper altar, that for seventy years and more has resisted the perversion of their creed, and yet loved King and Queen. Held all their lands despite rapacious challenge. Seen the storm of Protestantism rising, like a thousand white horses on Baltimore Strand, and resisted. My head is bare to her, my heart is open, she strikes my crown and stabs me through. I wish, Dallas Sweetman, you had never found her on the beach, and that the pirates might have had her.

Dallas But I knew this speech was false. His mind was aching with that awful fear, that piercing sword, when a man of strong belief is asked to bend.

But bend he could not.

Lucinda Mountifort took me from the sea, as the sea started to devour me. I saw his love in his long face, and for my part loved him just as fiercely, simply. When it was to be a choice between him and my father, my heart parted like an apple, one half was all Mountifort, but the other half was thrown into the mire, to be stamped on by devils. But there is a rightness in the fog of things, and I followed the sound that spoke of rightness. He was my love, ordained in some long ago. It was a woman's love, grown and complete, a yearning and a confusing delight. I could not have enough of him, like a luxury sent from afar in small quantities, even as I kissed him I starved for more kisses. My love was famishing and fulfilling all in one. But the word that came from my father, of distress and pain, was like that owl that sounds his one note over the boglands in the night, sweet and terrible, and something in me heeded it, and something in me prevented me going. I loved my father in infinite measure, and yet there was a greater infinity in my love for Mountifort, and his for me. He was just a tall, long-faced, easy, ordinary man, that seemed to me the definition of celestial all the same. And that is the force of human love, transmuting, instructing, bidding.

Dallas Lucinda was sent a notice not to come home, to stay where she was, wherever that was. Moreover, there would be no question of a dowry, as Lucius would disinherit her immediately.

By this means he hoped to cool her. That she might return contrite, begging for mercy and forgiveness. Lucius was certain the evil prelate – whose name we now knew was Mountifort Longfield, a well-born man enough for all that – would not wish to marry a beggar. The priest was the messenger in it all.

Lucius presumed the rescuer of his daughter a villain, because of his unholy cloth.

In this he was wrong. I was told that Mountifort Longfield laughed, as was his wont, and said she would do as the angel she was, which was a person beyond price.

Lucius dismissed the priest, who had to slink back to Lisbon to God knows what fate, to endure the wrath of the Princess of Brazil.

Lucius dons his great cloak.

You will wish to be told that Lucius came through this sorrow, and some great boon came to him to save his heart. It was not so. He put all his lands and buildings in order, went over the bay to Sherkin, and fell from the great cliff there in a darkling night.

Mrs Reddan Oh, foul, most foul. I am amazed at this vile history.

Lucius sits on the ground, the cloak spreading about him.

Dallas Three days I lay in that very selfsame room where I had hid his children all those years before. I lay upon the selfsame bed, with its withered peltings, and wept. I wept for poor Lucius, that kingly, kindly man.

Now foul Mrs Reddan was to be queen of everything, and that I could not bear. I packed my few sticks and books, and set out for Cork.

Mrs Reddan appearing.

Mrs Reddan Oh, let me set this to rights.

At length Lucinda came home. At the harbour of Rosscarbery she fell into the water and was rescued by a young man in holy orders. He risked his own life by jumping in to save her, and for this she gave him her very love. It was difficult vexing news for Lucius. In the first part, as a Protestant she would lose her Portuguese inheritance. In the second, he worried for her immortal soul. Yet Lucius was kind above all. He went to see her. Although with me he expressed a violent choler, yet when Lucinda showed the man to him, and asked for his forgiveness and his blessing, Lucius after much debate and vexatious thinking obliged. She already had her golden equipage, and Lucius added five thousand pounds to her dowry. Her husband we knew would have taken her with nothing, but I am sure was well pleased with this progression.

Lucius We must learn how to live in Ireland. Old ways are weakening and there must be new. My happiness has been recomposed by my new wife. Likewise, my darling Lucinda, may it be with you. Be both Catholic and Protestant, Old and New English, and in all regards a child of this country, and may we all be happy. Our country is uncertain and tumultuous. God protect us, and bless our future and our progeny.

Mrs Reddan On Lucius's return, disappeared Dallas Sweetman from our estate.

Music.

Dallas There was fierce rage in me. All the long road, as I urged my pony on, I thought of my perfect master, and resolved to kill this man that had murdered him and all his world.

Mrs Reddan Your words no longer bear anything in them except a general misery and sorrow.

Dallas When the name Lucinda was on my lips, I spat, and cursed her.

I called her a harlot to the old Cork skies, and gave thanks to God her mother had not lived to see this sundering of her faith, the purpose of their lives undone.

Mountifort Longfield had a handsome house, and a glebe of some rapacious Protestant lord. It was situated at the edge of that great city, with its own orchard and lawns and sharp-cut hedges.

Easy as an innocent I approached the house, and told who I was, and asked to see my lady.

I must have seemed so quiet, gentle, true, that there was seen to be no trouble in it, and I was brought up to her room to talk with her.

Mountifort and Lucinda seated, like an emblem of marriage.

There she sat with Mountifort by her. I walked in a door one kind of man, but when I saw her, I was entirely changed.

She looked like a ghost, a wraith, a blowing flower.

No substance had she, with sunken face, her young eyes so blue but rimmed with sooty black. Mountifort Longfield held her arm, as if for fear she might fall from her chair without support.

She asked me in broken voice the story of her father. I told it true, but simple and short, not to add to her signalling pain. I told her also that he loved her to the last, and spoke ever softly of her. That he did not kill himself for her, but because he had lost his wits, a thing, I said, long gathering, I believed, having watched him these last years.

Her listening face.

As I spoke, the poison rose up from her skin, it seemed, and a tiny faint blush of pink touched again on her cheeks, like slight, first flowers in the prime.

He embraces her.

You will say, my judges, I did wrong.

Why did I not tell the truth, and cast down and blight her as a blasphemous witch?

But, my judges, so soft was she, so slight, so ruined, I could not but put her together again, if I could.

Mountifort gets up and embraces Dallas.

Mountifort Longfield, himself a gentle man, rose from his place, walked down the long scrubbed floor, and to my amazement, took me in his arms.

I had never been embraced so strange before, a thought from the great distant past assaulted me, and I remembered my own father doing so, before the days of his ruin.

What a strange matter it was.

Mrs Reddan (*shaking her head, quietly now*) You lie.

Dallas Mountifort Longfield, that deadly man, as I had thought, in the moment that he thanked me, returned to me a vision of my lost father.

I was received into the household as a valued man.

I was more than servant then. Mountifort was interested in my birth, he too had cousins in the Barony Forth of Wexford, and knew that ancient story, of Englishness alive and fostered in that place. For the first time since young manhood I felt myself to be a man, a personage of some weight, a living heart.

In many things he consulted me from that day forth, and always looked to me for special wisdom, though wisdom I had not. Such was the ways of Mountifort Longfield, the very ways that Lucinda of course had seen, even as she knelt on the quay.

Yes, yes, and I changed my cloth. I turned my blessed coat. I thought, if Lucinda is to be Protestant, so must I.

What a fearing change was that?

Would I not burn in that Catholic Hell, my soul boil like an onion in that vast soup of human tears? I supposed it might. Yet was I willing to cross over, against all the centuries of my sort, because – because my life in the human present was given back to me.

And no, Lucinda was not immune to age. She aged as we all do. Nor no children as a blessing given. She narrowed and paled with the years, her first beauty rubbed out like a final gold line on an evening landscape.

She rose into a different beauty, that a civil face may keep, a more perfect beauty because made by the hiding soul itself.

And if she was to be old, how much older I? Grievous and withering, with 'shrinking shank' indeed.

But what of that truly?

Oh, Lucius died, but also, not many years later, died away all his world, the signs and wonders of his kind, vanishing away in slaughter and hindrance, like many in Ireland before them, in the long and painful turning of time.

But I have seen great goodness on the earth of Ireland, and that is no little thing. I saw Lucius Lysaght, the finest of Catholics, deal in the world with grace. And his daughter Lucinda, peerless Protestant, show her light to the wondering world.

And though I am small, and dark, and of no import, I gauge the width of my own self by these things.

Saying, these matters I saw for myself on the earth, these matters I witnessed, and puzzled for myself.

In Ireland, that puzzle which cannot be puzzled out – and may God commend it.

And as I teeter here on the edge of some second death, and wait for God the great pirate of Araby to fetch me off, and talk to you, my friends, my judges, I commend you all to God.

And commend all Englishmen in Ireland to Him, and all who deserve it, as I may myself.

Dallas stands in silence.

Have I spoken fully? Have I spoken well?

Mrs Reddan In your faces he throws his watery truth.

His story, his history, cancels out his soul, he is rescinded, burned away, like a wishbone in a bonefire, where the truth is flames.

Lucinda and Mountifort had not many days of happiness. For soon Mountifort Longfield was found slain. Some secret man, as first we thought, in rage and anger, seeming to approach Lucinda's husband with gladness and cheer, came close to him, all close, like a friend or a brother, and drawing a short sword that he had hidden in his coat, drove it into the reverend gentleman to the hilt, murdering him in cold and terrible murder.

Yes, yes, Dallas Sweetman.

The murderer fled away, nor was found again in the general mire of Ireland.

Lucius withered and thinned, till his face had the skin of the flower Honesty. The sorrow and grieving of his daughter famished him.

She vanished also from our ken. News came now and then of her being sighted in some vicinity, she seemed to thread her way through the English towns of Ireland, asking here and there her patient, terrible question. She was seeking a man and, item by item, described him where she went. For years she journeyed, even as Elizabeth died and James came to the throne. But great matters of history were nothing to her now. I imagined her growing ragged and dark, an image of avenging love, ever looking for the murderer of her husband.

My lovely old Lucius, bent with horrid care, rowed in his gristled strength a little skiff out to Sherkin Island, must have walked in some state of perplexity to the cliff, and from there fell.

An act of murder just as sure as if Dallas Sweetman had put that same sword into his heart.

Speak, speak, Dallas, the darkness is falling round these ancient roofs, night's old cloak thrown casually round us, speak now, speak now.

Dallas My story – my history. That I undertook to tell you. As proof of my innocence. And of Mrs Reddan's lies.

It seemed true as I spoke it. It did. In many respects was true.

But my mouth is full of ashes.

My judges, you have paid heed to me, conferred on me I think the compliment of belief.

I thank you.

Is not God also in this great hull of stone, this passing ship that does not pass, this rearing place that clenches to the earth? He is, He is, may He protect me.

I hear the roaring of the waterfall, right enough, and taste the mist that it engenders. I am to fall.

But so –

With angry heart I went to Cork, just as I said.

I had my sword nesting in my cloak.

Mountifort Longfield rose up, just as I said, oh yes, oh yes, to greet me. God give me that scene again in reality, so I may change it, but even He cannot.

Yet I would still go back, ask old Father Time to wend back that way with his scythe, leading me along the road, go back, go back, speaking all language backwards, telling all stories backwards, till we reach again that moment, when I might have shown – not mercy exactly.

The love I owed her, as the owner of my heart.

I drew out my sword, his face opened in amazement. He spread his arms, it was as if to welcome my thrust, how could that be? He neither ran nor feinted sideways. He uttered a prayer to his God. This put more rage in me. And he opened his palms towards me.

I drove in the sword, I hacked at him as he fell, and broke his head.

I killed him, killed him, that good man.

The true love of the woman that I loved.

I fled from that place of ruin, Lucinda's calling, crying voice behind me, tying about my soul in twines of iron.

Mrs Reddan Oh, foolish, broken, mortal man.

Dallas And Lucius killed himself, after, *after* I left his house, and I had done my work against the gentle reverend. I can well conjure why. He will have thought that, in speaking against Mountifort in my presence, in such raging terms, he had inadvertently seemed to commission me to kill him, and had destroyed his daughter's happiness thereby – no repentance enough for that.

That was the infinite discrimination of his mind.

And if that is also to my charge, I accept it, and take his life also as a cancellation on my soul.

No repentance enough – and still to live.

God strike me down, condemn me, break me under His holy heel, unable to forgive, unable to forgive.

This I know.

My judges. My judges.

I fled away, to find such wilderness where only wolves would live, and men like wolves, all those wide and lonely tracts of Ireland, where it is dangerous even for a robin to alight and seek a worm. And there for a long time I roamed, dirtied and ragged, with a lengthening beard, till I was a very wolf myself, worthy only of slaughter.

Weeks, months later, I hardly knew the why, I asked benediction of one of those new priests, of the new faith, and turned my coat, in hopeless hope to be something of what she was.

To be at length, at least, close to her in Heaven.

Then coming into a little dirty village, somewhere near Baltimore as it happened, by my old districts wandering, and stopping for an hour in a low drinking-house, I heard my own story in the mouth of a stranger, how Lucius had died, and how his daughter sought everywhere the killer of her love.

And that seemed a dark miracle, till I thought, it is now the first-told story of this place, casually told to all.

For all suffering becomes at length a mere story, as a mocking afterlife of all our pains.

'I shal tellen thee a feithful tale,' quod he.

The stranger, not knowing me, told the tale as you might a fable, or a little handful of cindery lies.

But it was all truth, I knew.

Terrible, hurting, killing truth.

Mrs Reddan There, in his mouth, at last, the wakening coal of truth, red on his trembling tongue, burning and mining down into his throat, to touch his foul heart, brambled and cut by his deeds. Now I can nest in silence, tuck my coat, and go, and wander back across those fields I do not know, the neat cold farms of this Kent, and dwindle away, a figure in the distance, till distance snuffs me out. Not the victory I envisaged as we began, which was to see him sucked down before me into Hell, his lies packed back into his soul like fire, but I am strangely content.

There is sorrow enough everywhere in this tale to engender in me the glimmer of forgiveness.

A mystery.

She goes.

Dallas After that, I went looking for her. It was strange to be looking for someone I knew was looking for me, to dispatch me. But, I could not find her. Maybe an old man can find no one. An old man, like an old house with one last light in it. My desire was not to explain, not to be forgiven, but to be near her. So she could do as she wished, and desired, do what was proper to her. Because that was all that remained of me, the last tincture of myself, and maybe in the upshot the truest part of me, my love for her.

I am to be swallowed up in Hell, to cry out like Jonah in the fiery smithy of the whale.

And yet as I burn in the eternal flame, something of me will burn harder, brighter, my love, my laughable, ruinous and unnoticed love.

From far off appears a glimmering figure, which starts the long walk down to him through the body of the cathedral. Music.

It's a woman in her travelling cloak.

When she reaches Dallas, she pulls down the hood.

Lucinda I am Lucinda Lysaght, do you know me?

Dallas Yes, yes, I am your servant.

She reveals a sword under the cloak, raises it above him.

Lucinda I will strike you, Dallas, for the safety of your soul. You have done such wrong to me, you whom I loved as a child, you who watched over me, who taught me all the mysteries and the wonders, of the stars and the sun, of the Greeks and the Carthaginians, the rising and the falling of men and empires, of all human things.

Dallas looks up at her, spreads his arms, and turns the palms towards her.

Dallas Lucinda, Lucinda. I welcome it. It is just.

Lucinda You are in every way beyond justice, Dallas, for what you did to my beloved.

Dallas No man is beyond justice, though he may lie out on the margins of forgiveness, as I do myself. But I look in over the human fields, and yearn to be there again.

Lucinda I have searched for you and searched for you, I have looked in cabins and in little cities, I have asked for you by name, and drawn your face, and shown it, and searched and searched.

Dallas And all the while I went out to find you.

Lucinda Why to find me, when you knew I would have you dead?

Dallas That I might stand near you again, and see your face, just for a moment. The wren flies into his nest, in a twinkle. I desired only so much time.

Lucinda You see my face now. Are you satisfied? Before I bring this sword down on your head?

Dallas I am satisfied. I have done you wrong so great I believe you are just in your action. By your action now you may bring me back into the book of life. But the stranger thing is, this great happiness in me, just to see you. Your face radiates for me like a country lamp, like the sun in childhood, like the fire of my parents, like my favourite word, like the robin's wife to the robin when she returns in the summer.

Lucinda Your happiness is unwelcome, ridiculous, disgusting. You destroyed my own. You killed Mountifort Longfield, my husband.

Dallas I did. I confessed to that, you know?

Lucinda Do you boast of your contrition?

Dallas May God forgive me. You need not. Strike me down. If it is what fits the crime, what must be done, let it be done.

Lucinda You are almost brave. I took you for a creeping coward now, all changed and ruined, but I see there is something of Dallas Sweetman in you still, that kindly servant of my father's, whom I loved.

Dallas I have been made braver by being made smaller, by the wearing down of the wheel of living, the great grindstone of God which grinds us, till we are only dust for a loaf. Strike me.

Lucinda Do not ask me to strike you. Resist me. Cower before me, cry out for life, beg me for forgiveness, creep and crawl, let me take your much-desired life for the much-desired life you took. In my head I carry him, in my heart I bear him, in my soul I have him nesting. And still, and still I know there is nothing there, because you made nothing of him. You saw him, ordinary and simple in his life, and put in this sword where his living self was beating, and destroyed him. So that my face cracked, my bones became slivers, my hands became hooks of torture, you laid on my backbone a great tonnage of grief, and I died at waking, and died at sleeping, it was all deaths with me, for the loss of him. The one perfect answer to my human question, the wood pigeon that answered my wood pigeon's call, co-co-co-rico. To be endlessly sounded now, till the woods have fallen, the sky has burned out to black, and the earth is a cinder in the hearth of God, and it is all gone, all love, all present feeling, all future of laughter, all future of tears, till the last thing left is the cry of a woman, all her loves taken from her, a last cry, till God presses it smaller and smaller, till it is gone, infinitely gone, but still at the heart of it, the very heart of nothing, the invisible centre, my grief, my grief. Lay out your bare head to be killed.

Dallas Like so, like so? Is this crawling enough? I have seen you, and now need no more life. I am content. I am ready to go. Like old St Thomas, I desire it.

Lucinda raises the sword higher as if to bring it down on his head, Dallas closes his eyes, waiting, waiting, but at the last moment she seems to lose her strength and lets it fall clattering onto the ground.

(*Wearily.*) Rise up, Dallas Sweetman, I cannot kill you now.

Rise up, rise up.

She almost has to reach down and help him up. He gets to his feet.

I am too weary. I have a long way to go. I cannot go alone. I cannot. Will you follow me? Will you be my servant again?

Dallas (*utterly surprised, and eager*) I will, I will.

Lucinda Though we walk through the woods of wolves, though we pass through the mires of demons and saints?

Dallas No matter, I will.

Lucinda Through the fields of blood, through the halls of difficult histories, will you follow me?

Dallas I will.

Lucinda And what of human love, the darkest mire of all, will you follow me through that?

Dallas I will. I will gladly.

She touches his arm, exhausted.

Lucinda Then, follow me.

They hold there a few moments. Music.

They go, Dallas following Lucinda.

End.